MOVIE NOVEL

BY JUDY KATSCHKE

BASED ON THE SCREENPLAY BY JOHN A. DAVIS

SCHOLASTIC INC.

New York   Toronto   London   Auckland   Sydney

Mexico City   New Delhi   Hong Kong   Buenos Aires

No part of this publication may be reproduced in whole or in part, or stored in a retrieval system, or transmitted in any form or by any means, electronic, mechanical, photocopying, recording, or otherwise, without written permission of the publisher. For information regarding permission, write to Scholastic Inc., Attention: Permissions Department, 557 Broadway, New York, NY 10012.

First publisihed in the UK by Scholastic Ltd, 2006
Scholastic Children's Books, Euston House,
24 Eversholt Street, London NW1 1DB, UK

ISBN 0-439-85683-3

12   11   10   9   8   7   6   5   4   3   2   6   7   8   9   10/0

Printed in the U.S.A.
First printing, July 2006

ONE

Like most days, it was a busy day at the anthill.

A long line of forager ants were carrying a variety of food items — sticks, bug parts, crumbs — into the mound to feed the colony. The wrangler ants were herding a group of caterpillars into the caravan. Each ant had his own task that together helped to keep the ant colony running smoothly.

Once down inside the anthill, the ants carried their finds through tunnels and bustling chambers.

In the hatching chamber, busy nurse ants ran back and forth catching babies as they popped out of their cocoons. Each baby ant — or pupa — was born with antennae, a mandible, a thorax, and a job to do.

"Soldier!" one nurse shouted as her pupa hissed and pawed.

"Scout!" another nurse called as her baby turned its head from side to side, looking around.

One little pupa barfed all over his nurse.

A no-brainer! "Regurgitator!" his nurse called out.

POP! Another cocoon burst open. A pretty young nurse named Hova caught the baby and rocked it in her arms.

"Who's a good boy?" Hova cooed.

The head nurse ant sighed. Hova was a very caring nurse. But did she have to care for the whole ant colony?

"We've got two thousand more births today, Hova," the head nurse said. "Just pick a task group. Soldier? Worker? Which one?"

"It's hard to just label an ant on a first impression," Hova said.

The head nurse's six arms filled with falling babies. Hova was holding up the assembly line!

"Hova!" she shouted. "Hurry up!"

Babies wailed as chaos erupted in the hatching chamber. It didn't stop Hova from cuddling with her catch.

"You remind me of someone," Hova whispered to the pupa.

That someone was only a few chambers away. His

name was Zoc, and while hundreds of ants slept peacefully after a hard day, he was working overtime.

"Hmm," Zoc said, probing the cave walls with his antennae. His body was decorated with colorful paint and he held a tribal staff. Zoc was a wizard ant, searching for the final ingredient for a magic potion.

Zoc felt something behind the wall. "That's it!" he said. "Spindle! Light!"

Zoc's pet glow mite, Spindle, aimed his glowing butt toward the wall. As Zoc chipped away at the wall with his staff, chunks of dirt and rock showered down on the sleeping ants.

"What are you doing?" one ant shouted. "We're trying to sleep down here!"

Zoc frowned down at the ants perched on their stalactites. What did he expect from a bunch of crabby drones?

"What's more important?" Zoc asked. "Me finding the ingredient for my potion and saving the colony, or sleep?"

"Sleep!" they all answered.

"I'll try to be quiet," Zoc said with a sigh.

He pointed his staff toward the wall. It hummed and glowed until — *POW!* A charge of static shot out, blasting a huge hole in the cave wall.

Zoc peered through the hole and gasped. Inside was a mother lode of sparkling crystals!

"At last!" Zoc cried. "Fire crystals. The final ingredient!"

"Hey, what's your problem? Leave us alone!" a furious ant shouted.

"Hey, lousy wizard!" another one snapped. "Your magic never works. Why don't you just forage and sleep like the rest of us?"

Zoc smiled. He was not going to give up that easily. He was very close to completing his life's work — saving the ant colony.

Outside, a long line of ants marched on.

Suddenly, a dark shadow loomed over the parade. The ants gulped. They stared up into the sky just as a gigantic human crashed down to the ground next to them.

"Atomic wedgie!" Steve yelled.

"No!" Lucas cried as he struggled from under the pile of neighborhood kids. "Cut it out! Ahhhh!"

The ants watched as the human boy's face lay next to them, scraped and dirty. Suddenly, an enormous eyeball opened and stared right at them.

"It's the Destroyer!" one ant called.

"Run for your lives!" came the voice of another.

The ants dropped their cargo and scattered in all directions. Some twitched their antennae, sending a warning signal through the colony. It reached the hatching chamber, where nurses juggled their screaming babies. Then it reached the sleeping chamber — and Zoc!

"The Destroyer!" Zoc gasped.

BOOM! A water missile slammed into the anthill. A powerful wave gushed through the colony, sending hundreds of ants racing through the tunnels. As they spilled out of the anthill, more exploding water bombs greeted them.

Hova reached the top of the anthill and looked around.

"Hova, get to the grass!" Zoc warned. "It's dangerous up here."

"But I've always wanted to see a human up close," Hova said. "I hear they're capable of speech like us!"

"They are *nothing* like us!" Zoc said adamantly.

Another water bomb exploded. Zoc looked up and saw a giant human blasting away with a water gun.

It was the Destroyer, and it was time to fight back!

Zoc's staff glowed as he waved it in the air. "Away, monster!" he shouted. "Or I'll use my powers to destroy you!"

The Destroyer shook out his empty water gun. Then with an evil grin, he turned toward the anthill. The ants gasped as he lifted his giant foot over them, ready to stomp!

Zoc froze. His potions were powerful, but they were no match for a giant sneaker.

"Run!" Zoc shouted.

The Destroyer brought his foot down on the anthill with a smash. Screaming ants shot up through the air as the mound exploded in a cloud of dirt.

Hova stopped running and glanced back. Maybe she could reach this human by appealing to his softer side.

"Human!" Hova called. "We mean you no harm."

Zoc ran back for Hova. What was she thinking?

But just as he was about to pull her away, a dark shadow shrouded them. It was the giant sneaker, and it was about to stomp on both of them!

"I guess he didn't hear me," Hova cried.

The two friends squeezed their eyes shut and prepared for doom.

TWO

"*Luuuucas!*"

Lucas Nickle's foot froze in midair when he heard his mom's voice.

"Peanut?" Doreen Nickle called from her bedroom window. "It's time to come inside now."

Lucas stomped his foot just inches away from the anthill. As he turned and walked away, the ants sighed with relief.

"Peanut? I think I got through to him!" Hova said. "What do you think, Zoc?"

"Destroyer!" Zoc muttered.

The ants went back to work.

Meanwhile, inside the Nickle household, Doreen and Fred Nickle were gearing up for some serious rest and relaxation.

Doreen danced around the room as she tossed clothes into her open suitcase. Fred was already dressed for fun in the sun in his Hawaiian shirt and Bermuda shorts.

"Happy anniversary to us!" Fred sang. He grabbed a pair of bright swim trunks and pulled them over his head.

As Fred paraded around the room, their teenage daughter Tiffany walked by. Sixteen-year-old Tiffany had blond hair, a closet full of cutting-edge clothes, and a cell phone that was practically fused to her ear.

"Marcie," Tiffany murmured into her cell phone. "Check it out!"

SNAP! Fred froze like a deer in headlights as Tiffany took a picture with her camera phone.

Busted!

"Double my allowance or this goes straight on the Internet," Tiffany said as she held up the embarrassing photo.

"Done." Fred gulped.

The doorbell rang and Fred hurried downstairs. He swung open the door and groaned. On his doorstep was the shadow of a man surrounded by a swarm of buzzing flies. It was Stan Beals, the exterminator — again!

"I told you," Fred said. "I'm not interested!"

"You're new to this area," Stan said as he began to close the front door. "If I may be frank, this place is infested. But one signature can change that."

Stan blew puffs of cigar smoke at the flies, sending them crashing to the ground.

"I'm kind of busy," Fred said. "So if you don't mind . . ." He gestured toward the driveway.

"Nice hat," Stan said as he walked away.

Fred blushed as he pulled the swim trunks off his head. He needed a vacation — now!

"Lucas! Tiffany!" Doreen called from the kitchen. "We're leaving!"

Lucas sat on the floor of the living room, his eyes glued to his favorite electronic game, Frog Flyer. He grinned as the flying mallets attacked the hang-gliding amphibians. Smashing frogs was almost as fun as smashing ants!

"Why didn't you answer, Lucas?" Doreen asked as she stepped into the living room. She peeked behind the chair where Lucas was hiding and gasped.

Lucas's cheek was scraped, his hair was tangled, and his clothes were a dirty mess.

"Are you alright, sweetie?" Doreen asked.

Before Lucas could say anything, Fred answered, "Of course he's alright. Just a little roughhousing with your friends, right, Luke?"

Doreen didn't buy it. She reached down and wiped Lucas's face. "Are you sure you're okay, sweetie?"

"I'm fine," Lucas said. "Like Dad said, I was just playing with my friends."

"Like you've got any friends," Tiffany added. "He's so antisocial."

Fred looked out the window to see Steve and his posse of bullies riding Lucas's bike down the street. Doreen joined Fred at the window. She became more concerned.

"Maybe we shouldn't go on vacation, Fred?" Doreen added.

"Come on! It's our big wedding anniversary and we're going to Puerto Vallarta for a little quality time," Fred protested.

"I'm fine, Mom. Don't cancel your vacation just because of me. I can solve my own problems," Lucas declared.

"What problem?" Doreen said softly. "Bed wetting is nothing to be ashamed of, Peanut."

"What! I don't have any problems except for you treating me like a baby," Lucas snapped. "And stop calling me 'Peanut.' Everybody just leave me alone."

And with that, Lucas picked up his Gameboy and stomped off to his room.

Later, Lucas and his sister walked out on the porch and watched their mom and dad drive off.

"*Adios, mi familia!*" Fred called from the car.

"Whatever," Tiffany grumbled.

"Bye, Tiff! Bye, Lucas!" Doreen called as she waved. "I love you!"

Lucas folded his arms across his chest. He didn't wave back or say good-bye.

"You kids mind your grandma!" Fred said.

The car shot off. As black exhaust fumes spewed from the tailpipe, a window on the second floor flew open. A gray-haired lady dressed in sweats stuck out her head.

"Have fun! Don't worry — we're gonna make cookies!" she shouted. "And we're going to prepare for an alien attack."

Then she added, "You're poisoning the planet, Freddie! Stop global warming! Aaaack!"

Lucas jumped as his grandmother's false teeth clattered to the ground. It wasn't the first time it had happened. Mommo was always getting worked up over something — and losing her teeth in the process.

"Your turn." Tiffany sighed.

Lucas carried Mommo's teeth upstairs to her room. When he walked inside, he saw that the room was filled with power supplies and a dozen swirling fans.

"What are you doing?" Lucas asked.

"Preventing alien abduction," Mommo said as she popped her teeth back in. "Aliens hate air flow. It drives them nuts. We've gotta be prepared! Tell your friends!"

"I don't have any friends," Lucas said. "I look after myself."

THREE

"I, Zoc, call upon the elements!" Zoc bellowed. "The wind that blows! The rain that falls! The fire that burns!"

Zoc stood in his laboratory holding two fire crystals above a vial of purple liquid. Flames flickered off twisted roots that hung from the ceiling.

"Deliver your awesome power and transform my potion!" Zoc declared. "Klak Teel!"

Hova and Spindle watched as Zoc knocked the two crystals together. Instead of a mighty explosion, all they heard was a fizzle and a burp. And all they saw was a tiny puff of yellow smoke.

"Craznox!" Zoc yelled. He threw the crystal across the room. "The potion is supposed to change color! It's not changing color! It's not changing color!"

But Zoc refused to give up. He grabbed two more crystals and held them high. "I call upon the elements — wind, rain, etcetera," he babbled. "Transform my potion! Klak Teel! Klak Teel! Klakity Klak!"

He clacked the crystals together, but the only result was another tiny puff of yellow smoke.

Hova smiled at Zoc. He was working too hard, even for an ant! "Let's get some sleep," she said.

"But, Hova!" Zoc said. "We were almost squished today! I am so close to finding a solution to . . . to . . ."

Zoc's voice trailed off. He saw Hova walking over and holding a dandelion thistle. Zoc gulped when he saw the fluffy weed. The last thing he needed was a tickle attack!

"No!" Zoc cried. "Stop! Stop! Not the thorax!"

Hova giggled as she chased Zoc around the lab.

"I'm glad you two have something to laugh about," a voice cut in sharply.

Zoc and Hova spun around. Standing in the doorway, splashed with tribal paint, was the mackdaddy of ants. It was the big cheese! The —

"Head of Council!" Zoc gasped. "Um . . . I was just working on an experiment."

The Head of Council nodded at the dandelion. "Yes, I see," he said.

"How may I be of service?" Zoc asked humbly.

"Attacks from the Destroyer grow more frequent," the Head of Council said. "Most of our food supplies are gone. The Council was hoping you might have a solution."

Thinking for a moment, Zoc knew there was only one solution to save the colony from possible destruction. Their survival called for drastic measures.

"We must fight back! We must stop the Destroyer!" Zoc declared.

"A war?" Hova gasped. "But thousands of ants would be hurt! Perhaps if we could *communicate*. You know just, just talk with the human. . . ."

"Oh, that's a great idea! Let's have a nice chat!" Zoc mimicked Hova. "Well, hello, Destroyer. Gee, you look kinda tired. Why don't you just rest your enormous feet on my friend!"

Hurt by Zoc's remark, Hova turned away. "Sometimes you're a real stinkbug."

The Head of Council considered Zoc's solution. "A war with the human is impossible!"

"A wizard knows no such word!" Zoc said.

The Head of Council left the laboratory. Zoc turned back to his crystals. He studied a flawed crystal he had been holding in his hand.

"Useless hunk of rock," Zoc muttered.

But Zoc was not about to give up on defeating the Destroyer. Because to an ant wizard, *nothing* was impossible!

FOUR

Lucas stared at his reflection in a puddle. Watering the lawn was just one of the many chores on his dad's list.

"Only ten more chores to go." Lucas sighed. He was about to turn his hose on a flower bed when he heard laughter. Turning, Lucas saw a bunch of kids playing across the street.

"Friends," Lucas grumbled. "Who needs them?"

He turned back to his reflection when — *BOOM!* The puddle exploded. Lucas was splashed with a wave of water. He turned to see Steve walking over with a handful of firecrackers.

Steve tossed another firecracker at Lucas. It exploded just inches away from his feet.

"Oh, sorry, Lucas," Steve guffawed. "I was aiming for the ant mound."

The bully and his crew circled around Lucas. There was a tall skinny girl, a kid wearing a football helmet, a short round kid, and a kid with a mullet haircut. And of course, there was Nicky.

"What do you want?" Lucas asked defensively.

"Well, I just wanted to apologize for dog-piling you yesterday," Steve said sweetly. "Right, guys?"

"Yeah, we're sorry," Nicky said in a mocking tone. "Really sorry."

Then Nicky started laughing maniacally. Steve poked Nicky in the side.

"Ow!" Nicky cried. "Why do you have to do that in public?"

Steve turned to Lucas and stuck out his hand. "So, friends?" he asked sweetly.

"Really?" Lucas asked hesitantly.

"Really," Steve replied.

"Well, OK," Lucas conceded.

Suddenly, Steve shouted, "Dog pile!"

Lucas grunted as the kids piled on top of him, squishing him to the ground.

"He fell for it again!" Steve laughed.

The kids rolled off, and Lucas wobbled to his feet. But his ordeal was not over yet.

"Think fast!" Steve said. He pulled out a firecracker and tossed it at Lucas.

"Whoa!" Lucas cried. He stumbled backward, landing on his butt in a mud puddle. As he braced himself for the blast, the firecracker fuse fizzed out.

A dud! Lucas thought, relieved.

His eyes narrowed as the gang ran from his yard. He jumped to his feet and grabbed the garden hose. But instead of turning it on the bullies, he turned it straight toward the anthill.

Deep inside the colony, Zoc studied his crystals. "That's it!" he said. "There are cracks in the crystal. Perhaps a coating of resin will solve the problem."

Zoc filled the cracks with the sticky substance. Then he held two crystals over a purple mixture, knocked them together, and shouted, "Klak Teel!"

FLASH!

A brilliant green spark appeared. Then the purple mixture began to glow.

"Th-th-that's it!" Zoc stammered. "The potion is complete. Praise the Mother!"

Clutching the potion, Zoc jumped on the table and danced. He had achieved his lifelong goal! He had created a weapon to help the ants against the humans!

Hova was about to join him when a huge wall of water burst into the laboratory. The wave knocked Zoc and the potion off the table. He watched in horror as the swirling waters carried his precious potion away!

"Noooo!" Zoc screamed.

"Zoc!" Hova cried out as she ant-paddled through the raging waters.

"Hang on, Hova!" Zoc shouted. "Spindle, save the potion! Quickly!"

FIVE

"Gotcha!" Lucas sneered.

He forgot all about Steve and his friends as he drowned out the defenseless anthill. As Lucas sprayed, a voice interrupted him.

"Hello."

Lucas looked up and saw a huge man standing in his yard. The guy was dressed in a red jumpsuit and a red cap. Flies buzzed around his head.

"I was about your age when I flooded my first colony," the man said. "Good times."

"Who are you?" Lucas demanded.

The man flipped Lucas his refrigerator-magnet card.

"Stan Beals is the name," he said. "Beals-A-Bug Exterminator. You must be the Nickle boy. Your dad ordered my services, but he forgot to sign the contract before he left. So he told me to talk to you . . . uh . . ."

"Lucas," Lucas prompted skeptically.

"Yeah, Lucas!" Stan said. He whipped out a pen and the contract.

Lucas stared at the document. How did he know this guy was for real? "Do you have any references?" he asked.

Stan smacked his own arm, squashing one of the flies that had been buzzing around his head. "There's one," he said.

Lucas liked the idea of dead bugs — especially ants. But he didn't like the idea of signing a contract for his dad.

"I don't think I should," Lucas said.

Stan practically snapped the pen in half. "You don't think you should?" he cried. "So who does your thinking for you — your *mommy*?"

Lucas felt his cheeks burn red-hot. He'd had enough of people making him feel like a dork!

"Give me that contract," Lucas snapped.

"A mature decision," Stan said. "Enjoy a world that's bug-free. Sign right here and leave the killing to me!"

Lucas took Stan's grimy pen and signed on the dotted line.

Meanwhile, deep in the flooded colony, the ants were struggling to save their lives while Zoc struggled to save his potion.

"Spindle?" Zoc called. "Where are you?"

Spindle floated by on the potion bottle, using it as a raft.

"You saved the potion, Spindle!" Zoc cried. "Someone is getting an extra moldy root tonight!"

Spindle grunted.

"OK," Zoc said. "Two moldy roots."

Zoc slipped the potion into the pouch on top of his staff. As he pulled the drawstring, he heard a low moaning sound. It came from behind a collapsed wall.

Zoc and Hova dug through the wreckage until they reached the Head of Council. The old ant was seriously hurt and unable to stand.

Hova's nursing skills quickly kicked in. "Easy," she said gently. "Take it slow."

Zoc's wizard skills kicked in, too. He pulled a

dry leaf from his pouch. "Eat this," he said. "The yucca leaf gives strength."

The Head of Council chewed the leaf. "That stuff is nasty!" he sputtered.

Hova and Zoc helped the Head of Council to his feet. Moans and groans filled the chamber as they checked out the rest of the devastation.

"To attack without a reason is barbaric." The Head of Council sighed. "But what can we do? We're lost."

"No!" Zoc said with a smile. "We're saved!"

Zoc reached into his pouch and pulled out the glowing golden potion. He held it high.

"A potion?" the Head of Council asked. "What does it do?"

Zoc flashed a sly smile.

"Just *watch*!" he said, a twinkle in his eye.

SIX

It was the middle of the night. The only lights in the house were flashes of lightning from a distant storm. And the only sounds were those of Tiffany mumbling in her sleep as though she were still talking into her cell phone. Mommo dozed in her rocking chair, dreaming of aliens.

"They came from Venus. . . ." Mommo muttered. "No! Not the nasal probe!"

As quiet as an ant, Zoc peeked into each room. The Destroyer had to be somewhere. Zoc scurried to the end of the hall, where he heard a funny beeping sound. He followed the sound into another room. His eyes popped open when he saw the Destroyer fast asleep in his human bed, clutching a giant electronic game.

As more lightning flashed through the room, Zoc and an army of ants darted across the floor. Holding

Oh, no! It's the Destroyer!

The Destroyer is really Lucas Nickle, a lonely boy who bullies the ants because they're smaller than he is.

Lucas's mom calls him inside to say good-bye before she and Lucas's dad leave for their vacation.

Back at the ant colony, Zoc, a wizard ant, is busy making a magical potion that he hopes will protect the colony from the Destroyer.

Lucas takes his ant bullying to the next level when he signs a contract with the exterminator, Stan Beals.

Later that night, the ants sneak into Lucas's bedroom.

Yikes! The potion shrinks Lucas to the size of an ant. He's smaller than a potato chip!

Back at the colony, the Queen tells Lucas his punishment for bullying the ants is to live among the ants and learn their ways.

One of Lucas's first ant challenges is the forager obstacle course.

Oh, no! Lucas realizes the exterminator will attack soon.
He has to stop him!

Lucas returns to his house with his new friends to try to cancel the exterminator.

Lucas's sister Tiffany almost crushes Fugax with the phone!

It isn't easy being an ant, especially when you have to spend the night in a frog's stomach!

Despite Lucas's efforts, Stan the exterminator shows up to wipe out the ants.

Lucas proves he's become an ant by saving his friend Hova during the battle.

The ants scare Stan away, and the colony is safe again.

his staff, Zoc climbed to the top of Lucas's bed. He scaled Lucas's mountainous body until he reached his final destination — Lucas's ear!

It was all systems go. Zoc pulled out the potion. Carefully, he poured a few drops into Lucas's ear canal. He held his breath as the precious drops disappeared into the dark cave of the enormous ear.

"Now all we do is wait," Zoc murmured.

Lucas continued to sleep peacefully. Until —

BOOM!

A clap of thunder made him jerk straight up in his bed. He couldn't understand why his heart was pounding and his face was sweating.

Must have been a bummer of a dream, Lucas thought.

Through a blurred haze he saw his glasses on the floor. Before reaching for them he squeezed his eyes shut and then opened them again. His blanket looked like a vast desert stretching out before him!

Lucas had the creepy feeling that something was wrong. He turned to see that an enormous mountain had sprung up behind him. Suddenly, he realized the mountain was actually his pillow. And his Frog Flyer game was the size of a school bus!

Lucas looked wildly around his room, and then it began to click. His things weren't the same size because *he* wasn't the same size. He was the size of an *ant*!

His heart thumping, Lucas raced down the endless runway of his bed. He toppled over the edge, landing with a crunch on an open bag of potato chips.

"Whooaa!" Lucas yelled as he slid across the floor on a runaway chip.

The chip hit a giant sneaker and flipped over. Lucas stood up, dazed and confused. How did this happen? Why did this happen?

"Human," a voice blurted.

Lucas whipped around. Through his enormous glasses on the floor he spotted an ant. A *super-size* ant!

"Come with us," the ant ordered.

Lucas screamed as an army of ants lifted him and carried him away. Down the hall, Mommo woke with a start.

"What was that noise?" Mommo hissed. "Aliens? Well, they're not going to take *this* family!"

She grabbed her binoculars and a flashlight and peered out into the hallway. Her beam of light hit the line of ants marching toward the staircase. She could see them carrying something across their backs. Or *someone*!

"Help!" Lucas shouted. "Let me go!"

"Ahhhhhh!" Mommo screamed. She dropped her binoculars and slumped against the wall, feeling faint.

"They're here," Mommo mumbled as she slid down the wall. "Get me the President. . . . Def con four. . . . Yes, King of Mars, I will marry you. . . ."

The ants carried a kicking and screaming miniature Lucas out of the house and across the yard. When they reached the top of the anthill, they dumped Lucas down the hole.

"Ahhhhhh!" Lucas yelled.

His trip through the tunnels was like an extreme roller-coaster ride. He felt as if he was riding on a trail of ants through a House of Horrors! As Lucas shot through the sleep chamber, ants blasted him with larvae silk shooters. Then he tumbled into the hatching chamber, where he was plopped into the arms of a nurse.

"Scout? Soldier? Destroyer!" she screamed.

Lucas rode down the ants' backs until he reached

the end of his perilous journey — the ant city. Curious ants crowded around him to gawk and whisper.

"It's a human!" one ant declared.

"It's Peanut the Destroyer!" another one shouted.

Lucas felt sick as two guard ants hauled him through the hostile crowd. They pushed him into a large room filled with thousands and thousands of ants.

"Who are you?" Lucas demanded. "What did you do to me? Let me go!"

The guards shoved Lucas before the Head of Council. The high-ranking ants had streaks of tribal paint all over their skeletal bodies.

No way can this be real, Lucas thought. *All I have to do is wake up from this dream. Yeah, that's it!*

"Human!" the Head of Council boomed. "You have been brought before the Council to face judgment for crimes against the colony."

Lucas blinked his eyes hard. This wasn't a dream. This was really happening!

SEVEN

Lucas stood in front of the assembly of thousands of ants.

"Read the charges," said the Head of Council.

Another ant councilman unrolled a scroll and began to read:

"This Human Destructor-Beast, hereafter referred to as 'Peanut the Destroyer,' did willfully and with malice and forethought *crush* the food storage chambers and flood all of the lower hatching chambers."

"What is your verdict?" the Head of Council asked.

"Guilty," said one member of the Council.

"Guilty," chimed in another.

"Guilty," shouted a third.

The Head of Council leaned forward.

"We have a unanimous vote of 'guilty.' Sentencing of the human will be handed down by the Queen herself."

The ants shut their eyes and rubbed their mandibles. It created an eerie whining noise throughout the chamber. Suddenly, a stunning ant who was much larger than the rest rose up from a wall of steam.

That's got to be the Queen, Lucas thought. *Great.*

"Greetings, my children!" the Queen said. "And to our proven enemy, a human who threatens the very existence of our colony." The Queen glared at Lucas.

"Look, I'm sorry!" Lucas said. "I won't stomp on your anthill anymore. And I won't use the hose."

The ants gasped at the word *hose*.

"How was I supposed to know that ants had feelings?" Lucas asked. "Or families? Or trials? You're all just a bunch of little ants!"

"I humbly suggest that the Destroyer be dissected and studied," Zoc said. "Thank you."

"I object!" Lucas shouted.

The ants went wild, clicking their mandibles. The noise was so deafening that the Head of Council had to pound on the table with six gavels — one in each hand!

"Order! Order!" he shouted.

The Queen raised her multiple arms, and the ants quieted down.

"We have a choice," she said. "We can destroy this human and make safe this day. Or we can change the nature of this human and create a brighter future for *all* ants."

Lucas didn't know what the Queen was talking about. All he knew was that the second choice sounded better than the first!

"Therefore, I sentence this human to live and work in the colony and to learn our ways," the Queen declared. "He must become an ant!"

Lucas's mouth dropped open. Did the Queen just say what he thought she said?

Zoc couldn't believe it, either. Living as an ant was a privilege — not a sentence!

"What if he does not become an ant, my Queen?" Zoc asked. "I mean, come on!"

"That would be regrettable," the Queen answered.

Lucas's knees felt like jelly. Dealing with Steve and his gang was a piece of cake compared to what was happening to him now!

"Who will teach him our ways?" Zoc asked.

"I will," Hova said, stepping forward.

"Hova!" Zoc exclaimed. "How can you take in this thing?"

"I took *you* in," Hova said indignantly.

"It is done!" the Queen declared. "Let us continue our work."

Lucas watched as the ants dispersed. That was it?

"How long am I going to be this small?" Lucas cried. "You can't keep me here. It's inhuman!"

The Head of Council looked at Lucas.

"Yes," he said with a grin. "It *is*."

EIGHT

The next morning in the hatching chamber, Lucas developed a plan. With one eye on Hova, he dashed from one cocoon to the next. Grabbing a piece of cobweb hanging from the ceiling, Lucas wrapped it around his shivering body.

"Where are you, Peanut?" Hova called. "It's time to start your training!"

Lucas reviewed the plan in his head. All he had to do was run past the guards, escape the anthill, not get eaten by anything, and make it to his house. When his mom got home, she would take him to Doctor Weisman and he would fix everything!

"Now!" Lucas whispered.

He dashed out from behind a cocoon and ran straight into Hova.

"There you are, Peanut!" Hova said cheerily.

"Ahhh!" Lucas screamed.

"There are a million things I want to ask you," Hova said. "Like when were you hatched?"

"You're going to eat me," Lucas said cowering. "Aren't you?"

"You do look soft and chewy," Hova joked. "But I promised the Queen I wouldn't."

"Cross your heart?" Lucas asked.

"Cross my heart," Hova said as she reached back and crossed her butt.

"I said cross your *heart*!" Lucas said.

"I just did!" Hova said.

Lucas stared at Hova. There was a lot about ants he didn't know. And there was a lot he didn't really want to know!

"I don't want to be an ant!" Lucas said. "And my name is *not* Peanut. It's Lucas."

"Well, Lucas," Hova said. "You have to learn to become an ant if you want to go back home."

"How am I going to do that?" Lucas asked.

"You have to find your place in the colony," Hova explained. "Do you have any special skills?"

"I got a high score on Frog Flyers," Lucas said with a shrug.

"OK. . . ." Hova said slowly. There was a lot about humans that *she* didn't know!

Lucas wanted to go home more than anything. So he decided to get with the program and find his place in the colony.

"Let's try foraging," Hova said. "The instructor is a personal friend of mine."

So that afternoon, Lucas found himself in his own yard for his first foraging class. The instructor's name was Kreela. Usually she was as tough as an army sergeant. But the sight of Lucas made her downright antsy.

"Peanut the Destroyer?" Kreela cried. "I had to move out of my nest because of you!"

"It's Lucas," Lucas muttered.

"Kreela, please," Hova begged.

Kreela looked Lucas up and down. She didn't understand the strange cloth he was wearing on his body, but for Hova's sake she decided to give him a chance.

"OK, Destroyer," Kreela said. "There are two teams, the Blue Team and the Red Team. You're on the Blue Team."

The ants on the Blue Team groaned.

"There are many kinds of ants," Kreela went on. "But we are foragers. And like everything in the colony, foraging is a team effort."

Blah, blah, blah, Lucas thought. *Let's get this over with so I can go home!*

"In this test, each team must run through an obstacle course and retrieve the Sweet Rock," Kreela said. "No ant gets left behind. And the first team back with the Sweet Rock wins!"

"Yai, yai, yai, yai!" a voice shouted.

Lucas watched as another ant charged out of the grass. The energetic insect pushed back his safari-style hat and turned to face the two teams.

"Isn't it true that scout ants lead an exciting life of adventure while foragers just walk around picking stuff off the ground?" he asked.

"Fugax!" Kreela shouted. She knew this swashbuckling scout well — too well!

A smaller ant raised his hand. "What kind of adventures does a scout ant go on?" he asked.

Fugax gestured for the ants to gather around him. "In my travels, I just journeyed far beyond the Great Flat Rock."

The ant classmates oohed and ahhed.

"You mean the street," Lucas added, unimpressed.

Fugax cleared his troat and continued. "Yes, the great flat rock where the humans ride in their giant metal cocoons!"

More ahhhhs came from the crowd. Lucas just rolled his eyes. "Cars," he said.

Lucas was stealing Fugax's thunder. Flustered, Fugax snapped, "Who the heck is this kid?!"

"Fugax, meet the Destroyer," Kreela replied.

"The Destroyer? You know you're much smaller in person. Are you sure you're you?"

Kreela quickly reminded Fugax of Lucas's identity by lifting his foot and sticking it into Fugax's face. It didn't take long for Fugax to remember, and he raced off in the opposite direction.

"Now, are there any other questions about the assignment?" Kreela asked.

"What's a Sweet Rock?" Lucas asked.

But instead of replying, Kreela just barked, "Go!"

The teams were off! The Red Team and the Blue Team raced toward the first obstacle. It was a muddy ditch they had to cross.

"Bridge!" the Blue Team shouted. "Hoo yah!"

The ants formed a bridge with their bodies.

"Come on, Destroyer!" a teammate called.

"Nah," Lucas said. "I can do this myself."

Lucas stepped back. Then he charged toward the ditch and took a flying leap. But instead of landing on the other side, he crash-landed in the mud.

The ants formed a ladder to help Lucas up. Lucas refused their help until he realized that the mud was actually quicksand!

"I need your help! I need your help!" Lucas shouted.

But the quicksand ditch was only the beginning. After the ditch, the Blue Team raced to the next obstacle — the Soda Straw Lake. The Red Team was already in the lead, forming Slinky-type springs to propel them from one straw to the next.

"Bye, losers!" the Red Team jeered.

"Hurry, human," a Blue teammate told Lucas. "You're going to make us lose."

"I've only got two legs!" Lucas complained.

The Blue Team sprung into action. It was a wild ride for Lucas as he rode the ant-spring. But somewhere between *boings*, he began to feel sick.

"Stop," Lucas said. "I think I'm going to be sick. . . ."

And with that, Lucas let go of the other ants. The ants snapped forward like a slingshot, sending Lucas flying through the air. He sailed over the Red Team, landing smack in front of a giant red jelly bean! He was the first one there!

"The Sweet Rock?" Lucas wondered.

"Alright, Lucas!" Hova called.

Following Lucas's example, the other ants went for the slingshot move. Soon the whole Blue Team was soaring through the air and landing next to Lucas!

"We're in the lead!" a Blue teammate cheered.

"Did we win?" Lucas asked as they gathered chunks of jelly bean.

"Almost," a teammate said. "We just have to get the Sweet Rock over the finish line."

"What finish line?" Lucas asked.

A flurry of ants ran past Lucas to a brick on the grass. Lucas watched as the ants climbed the brick's steep wall. It was just a brick, but to the newly shrunken Lucas, it towered over him like the Empire State Building!

"Yeah, right." Lucas groaned.

The Red Team climbed the brick, too.

"Hurry, Lucas!" a teammate shouted. "They're catching up."

Lucas jumped up and down next to the brick. But he couldn't get a grip.

"Rope, rope!" the ants chanted.

The ants formed a rope with their bodies and dropped down the side. "Climb up, Lucas! Hurry! Let's go!"

Lucas didn't even try. He tossed his chunk of jelly bean into the grass in frustration and turned and walked away.

"Red Team wins!" Kreela announced.

The Red Team celebrated their victory on top of the brick. The defeated Blue Team glared at Lucas.

Lucas was mad, too. He had tried hard to find his place in the ant colony, but he *wasn't* an ant. He was a human kid!

"Can I go home now?" Lucas demanded.

NINE

"Lucas, you did fine on the obstacle course," Hova reassured him. "You just need to discover the ant within yourself. You can start by picturing yourself with six legs."

Lucas groaned as he and Hova walked through the tall grass toward the anthill. Couldn't she see that this whole idea was crazy?

"How is that going to get me home?" Lucas asked. "Look at me. I am *not* an ant!"

Hova planted two of her arms on her hips.

"You think it's easy being the Destroyer's little helper?" Hova asked. "Zoc and the others are already upset with me."

"You worry about *you*," Lucas said as he brushed aside a tall blade of grass. "And I'll worry about me."

"Oh, Lucas." Hova sighed. "That's not the way ants are."

"That's the way *I* am!" Lucas said.

Hova stopped in her tracks. Her eyes glazed over and her antennae began to twitch.

"Hello? Earth to ant lady?" Lucas said, waving his hand in front of her face. "What's the matter?"

"They're coming!" Hova cried. "*RUN!*"

Hova grabbed Lucas's arm. The two raced like the wind through the grassy jungle. Lucas could hear a faint buzzing sound. It grew louder and louder as they ran.

"They're after the herd!" Hova shouted.

"What herd?" Lucas asked.

Hova pointed to the anthill. A herd of spooked caterpillar was bucking wildly. Wrangler ants worked hard at calming them down.

"Whoa, easy, girl!" one wrangler said.

Lucas saw an armored wasp swoop down from the sky. It was much bigger than an ant, and it looked like some sort of biomechanical war machine.

The wasp plucked a caterpillar and its wrangler from the ground.

"Tell the Queen I love her!" the wrangler shouted as the wasp lifted him into the sky.

A whole squadron of wasps landed on the

ground, attacking the ants and snatching up the caterpillars.

"Come, brothers!" Fugax shouted. "For the Queen and our colony! This shall be our finest hour."

As Fugax charged forward. . . . *BOOM!* He was trampled by a legion of soldier ants moving ahead to defend a herd of caterpillars.

"Well, maybe this isn't *my* finest hour," Fugax said as he picked himself up off the ground.

Lucas and Hova were caught in the middle of the turmoil. "Get to the grass!" Hova cried to Lucas as they raced for cover.

An army of soldier ants moved in to protect the caterpillars while Kreela and her foragers hurled huge boulders at the wasps.

POW! A hit!

"That's got to sting!" Kreela cheered.

Another wasp rose behind Kreela. It raised its stinger, ready to attack. Then suddenly — *POW!* A long stick knocked the wasp aside.

Kreela whirled around. Zoc had swung his staff at the wasp to save her. What a guy!

"Thanks," Kreela said.

But Zoc wasn't done yet. Using his staff, he battled the wasp like a martial arts hero. Then he blasted the wasp with his staff, causing him to howl in pain.

One wasp was down for the count.

But there were many more to go!

While soldier ants blasted the enemy with their silk squirters, Lucas and Hova ran toward the safety of the grass. They were almost there when a huge wasp dropped in front of them.

As the wasp eyed Lucas, Hova stepped between them. "Leave him alone!" she shouted, smacking him right on the nose.

The wasp stumbled back. His maw dropped open and he let out a terrifying roar.

"Ahhhhh!" Hova screamed.

Hova's scream drew Zoc's attention, but he was helplessly stuck in a crowd of panicked ants, unable to reach her.

Then Zoc spotted Lucas.

"Don't just stand there!" he shouted. "Help her!"

Lucas was torn. Should he run for the safety of the grass? Or should he stay and help Hova?

He panicked and ran.

Zoc watched with disgust as Lucas bolted. Leave it to a human to think about himself over others!

Not looking back, Lucas darted through the grass. He stopped running when he found himself surrounded by sharp fragments of broken glass. He moved carefully until a beam of light reflected off the glass, burning him on the arm.

"Ow!" Lucas cried.

He blinked his eyes, and suddenly he was surrounded by ugly wasp reflections in the pieces of broken glass all around him. It reminded him of the House of Mirrors at the Fun Park — but *without* the fun!

"Where are you, little bug?" a wasp jeered.

Lucas looked from one piece of glass to the next. Which wasps were real and which ones were reflections?

He got his answer as a real wasp burst through the glass and dove at him.

"Ahhhh!" Lucas screamed. He ran and ran until he crashed into a giant cylinder in the grass. It was one of Nicky's firecrackers!

The wasp was closing in. Lucas knew he had to do something fast. He looked at the firecracker, then at a fragment of glass. Then Lucas Nickle had the most awesome idea!

TEN

"Hurry up!" Lucas hissed. "Light!"

He held the broken glass toward the sun and aimed it at the firecracker. Then he blew on the fuse embers, hoping for a spark. Just as the wasp was about to strike —

POOF! The fuse ignited.

Lucas danced around the firecracker, teasing the wasp. When the fuse burned close, he dropped it and ran.

"Fire in the hole!" Lucas shouted.

Zoc came running just as the wasp climbed over the firecracker. A second later — *BOOM!*

Lucas whipped around and smiled. The firecracker was blowing the wasp sky-high.

"What was that?" a nervous wasp asked.

"It's buzz time!" the wasp leader declared.

Hova's wasp let her go. Then all the wasps fell into formation and flew off.

As the dust cleared, the ants raced to Lucas.

"Did you see that?" Fugax exclaimed. He turned to Lucas with his hat in his hand and spread his arms wide. "Now I know why they call you Peanut. You've got a brain the size of a *peanut!*"

"I take back everything I ever said about you, Destroyer — I mean, Lucas!" Kreela said.

"Thank you, Lucas," Hova said. "You saved us."

Lucas felt kind of guilty as the ants bowed down to him. He wasn't used to being a hero. And he wasn't sure he *was* a hero, either. He knew he should have helped out sooner.

"Um, yeah," Lucas said. "Sure."

A shaky Zoc stood up near the blast crater.

"Oh, wake up!" Zoc said. "The Destroyer saved himself. The rest of us just got in the way."

Hova ran to her injured friend. "Zoc, are you alright?" she asked.

"I think I'm OK," Zoc said, coughing dramatically. He was milking his injury for all it was worth.

Hova tended to Zoc until she saw Lucas rubbing

his arm. "Lucas, you're hurt!" she cried. "Zoc, do you have any Yucca sap? Lucas has a burn."

Zoc was burning, too — with anger!

"This is our enemy," Zoc said. "He doesn't save ants, he kills ants. Or doesn't that matter to you?"

Lucas was silent as Zoc stormed off. He hated that the wizard ant hated him, but he couldn't help that he was a human.

Later that day, Lucas made the best of life in the colony. He even decided to join the other ants for a meal in the eating chamber.

"Mmm," Kreela said. "That is some good honeydew!"

"Here," Hova said as she plopped some greenish globules in front of Lucas. "Try some."

Lucas eyeballed the green blob warily. Finally, he pulled off a piece and popped it in his mouth. As he chewed, his eyes lit up. The stuff tasted like green apple bubble gum!

"This is awesome!" Lucas said.

He scarfed down more and more honeydew. Then he noticed Fugax holding an empty plate behind a caterpillar. Is that where the honeydew was coming from?

The ants studied Lucas as he began to gag.

"I didn't know humans could change colors!" Fugax said. "He's as green as the honeydew!"

"Why do you call it honeydew?" Lucas gulped.

"Because we used to say, 'Honey, do you believe we eat this stuff?'" Kreela explained.

"Here," Hova said, holding up a brownish-green root. "This alka root will make you feel better. Zoc discovered its powers to expel evil and create well-being."

Hova mixed the root with water. It began to fizz.

"Zoc hates me," Lucas said.

"Zoc has anger issues," Hova agreed. "But he's a true ant. Hard on the outside, soft on the inside."

Lucas took the fizzy root and gobbled it down. After a few seconds he felt his stomach churn and he heard it rumble.

"Brrraaaaap!" Lucas belched loudly.

"The evil has left him!" Fugax declared. "Praise the Mother!"

The ants bowed down.

"Who is the Mother?" Lucas asked. "Is it the Queen?"

"The Ant Mother is the Queen of Queens!" Hova said.

"She gave birth to the first colony," Kreela explained. "She's the mother of all ants!"

"It is said that one day she will return," Fugax said. "And when she does, honeydew will pour from the sky like rain!"

Lucas wrinkled his nose. "It's going to rain caterpillar poop and you're happy about that?" he asked.

"Come on," Hova said, gently taking Lucas's arm. "It is time for you to see."

Lucas followed the ants through a long tunnel. It led to an enormous cavern.

"This is the chamber of the ages," Hova said. She pointed to a slew of drawings made by ants on the wall. "These drawings tell the story of our colony. Our history."

"This is the image of the Mother," Hova said, pointing to a huge hieroglyphic of a giant ant flying out of the sun.

While the ants bowed to the Ant Mother, Lucas turned to another drawing. It showed a humanlike figure with smoke billowing from his mouth and hands. Dozens of ants lay dead at his feet.

Lucas stared at it.

"What's *that* one?" he asked.

"It's the evil one!" Kreela said. "The Cloud Breather."

"No one is sure what it is," Hova said. "All we know is that death is said to follow it."

Lucas studied the drawing. There was something familiar about the guy. Where had he seen him before?

"The exterminator!" Lucas remembered. "I have to cancel him!"

Lucas began running from the chamber. "I've got to go home," he said. "Right now!"

"Lucas, wait!" Hova called. "You're not an ant yet!"

ELEVEN

"Please!" Lucas said. "Just a quick visit."

"No way, two legs!" Kreela said. "The human's nest is forbidden."

Lucas stopped running. He had to go home. But he couldn't tell the ants why.

"Um . . . the colony needs food, right?" Lucas asked.

"Food?" Fugax asked.

"Sweet Rocks," Lucas blurted. "My house is full of them!"

The ants traded looks.

"Let's go!" Fugax said.

Lucas, Hova, Fugax, and Kreela made their way out of the anthill, moving toward the Nickle house. They climbed up the front steps and slipped underneath the door. But when they saw the jungle of carpet stretched before them, they groaned.

"Why did Mom have to get *shag* carpet?" Lucas said. "It'll take days to get to the kitchen!"

Suddenly, Lucas saw a large fan blowing rose petals across the room. He had another brainstorm.

"Come on!" Lucas cried. He climbed up onto a table next to a vase of roses. Then he grabbed a fallen rose petal and held it high over his head, looking down at the whirling fan below.

"This is called hang gliding," Lucas explained. "When I give the word, everybody jump."

The ants looked nervously at one another. But then they each grabbed a rose petal and imitated Lucas.

Everyone waited until the fan swiveled toward them. At the first hint of wind, Lucas gave the word.

"Now!" he shouted.

The four tiny voyagers jumped off the table and — *WHOOSH* — the wind blew them straight toward the kitchen.

"Awesome!" Lucas cheered.

They sailed past the mantle and the Nickles'

vacation pictures from Hawaii and Egypt. Lucas proudly described the pictures and the family adventures to his new friends. As he flew past the photos, Lucas realized how much he missed his mom and dad.

Why didn't I tell Mom good-bye? He wondered. *How could I have been such a jerk?*

When Lucas and the ants reached the kitchen, they scrambled up on the counter. Lucas pointed to a jar of brightly colored jelly beans. It was the Sweet Rock mother lode!

"Let's eat!" Fugax declared. "I mean, let's get these back to share with the rest of the colony."

While the ants got busy foraging jelly beans, Lucas dashed to the refrigerator. He scanned the door for Stan Beals' enormous magnetic card and quickly memorized the phone number. Then Lucas jumped up and down on the phone buttons, dialing the exterminator's number. He stopped when he heard a loud *SLAM!*

"Mommo!" a voice shouted. "I'm home!"

"What was that?" Hova gasped.

"It's Tiffany," Lucas said. "Hurry up!"

Lucas listened to Tiffany's footsteps on the staircase. When the coast was clear, he continued jumping.

BEEP! BEEP! BEEP!

Lucas made a running jump for the last button. Though he didn't realize it, his feet had landed on the seven and the four at the same time.

BEEEEEEP!

"Hello!" Lucas shouted into the mouthpiece. "This is Lucas Nickle. I need to cancel my order."

Hova looked curiously at Lucas. What order?

"Cancel the contract!" Lucas shouted. "No exterminator!"

"No extra tomato," the voice on the other end said. "Got it! Thanks for calling Pizza Kingdom."

Lucas didn't hear the Pizza Kingdom part. All he heard was the click on the other end.

"Lucas?" Hova asked. "What's an exterminator?"

"Don't worry," Lucas said with a smile. "Everything is OK now."

The phone rang and Lucas jumped a mile high. He could hear someone approaching the kitchen.

"We've got to hide!" Lucas said.

Lucas and the ants scattered and hid under the toaster just as Tiffany bopped into the kitchen and picked up the phone.

"This is Tiff," she said. "Hi, Mom. Everything is fine. . . . Huh? . . . Lucas is in his room playing those stupid video games. I will. . . . I will. . . . OK, Mom."

Tiffany's eyes fell on a jelly bean moving mysteriously on its own on the kitchen counter. It was Fugax! He hadn't hidden with the rest of the gang.

Tiffany tilted her head as she looked closer, recognizing that it was an ant. Lucas and the others tried to wave at Fugax to stop, but he merely smiled and waved back, not seeing Tiffany.

"Ewwwww!" Tiffany shouted. "Ants!"

"You must be Tiffany. . . . Ahh!" Fugax cried. He bobbed and weaved as Tiffany swatted Fugax with the phone. After a few attempts, the phone crashed down on Fugax.

"No, Tiffany!" Mommo shouted. "You'll squish Lucas!"

Lucas peeked out from behind the toaster. He could see his grandma rushing into the kitchen.

Mommo grabbed Tiffany's phone and babbled into the mouthpiece. "Everything's fine," Mommo said. "Nobody shrunk. Bye-bye!"

"What are you talking about?" Tiffany asked.

Lucas and the ants scurried to the kitchen sink. Kreela helped a limping Fugax, whose leg had been injured by the phone.

When Mommo saw them diving down the drain, she ran to the sink and began to yell.

"Let him go!" she shrieked. "It's me you want! Probe me instead! *Lucaaaaasss!*" *CRASH!*

Mommo's giant teeth narrowly missed Lucas as he slid down the drain. He wanted to tell his grandma that aliens hadn't abducted him — ants had. But that would have to wait.

At least I canceled the exterminator, Lucas thought. *Mission accomplished.*

The ants escaped the house and hurried toward the anthill. Zoc was waiting near the mound, searching frantically for Hova.

"Are you alright, Hova?" Zoc asked.

"Of course," Hova said. "Why wouldn't I be?"

"Zoc, we went to Hawaii and the Pyramids," Fugax said. "Then we flew —"

"— we were inside the human's nest," Kreela cut in.

"Human's nest?" Zoc cried. "That's forbidden!"

"I know," Fugax said. "But it was filled with Sweet Rocks. A giant human appeared and some massive teeth narrowly missed us. But here we are!"

The ants disappeared into the anthill. Lucas was about to follow when Zoc blocked him with his staff.

Zoc pulled a vial of blue fluid from his pouch. "You know what this is?" he asked Lucas. Lucas shook his head.

"This is the potion that will make you big again," Zoc replied.

Lucas's face brightened and he excitedly grabbed for the vial. But Zoc was in no mood to be generous. He pulled it away, leaving Lucas empty-handed.

"Take a good long look at it, because this is the last time you will ever see it. You are a threat to every ant in this colony, especially Hova."

Lucas stared at Zoc. "I would never do anything to hurt Hova. I just want to go home," Lucas said.

"There is no way I'm ever going to make you big

again," Zoc said. "If I were you, I'd try to find help somewhere else."

Lucas's heart sank. He wanted to cry, but all he could do was walk away.

TWELVE

"Ouch! Ow!" Fugax cried. "Pain. Hurt."

It was the middle of the night in the sleeping chamber, and Kreela was about to apply a resin cast to Fugax's injured leg.

"You big pupa!" Kreela said. "I haven't even touched you yet!"

Zoc quietly slipped into the chamber. He didn't want anyone to see him, but he was out of luck.

"Zoc, where's Lucas?" Hova asked.

Zoc stared at Hova. How could he tell her that he had banished her precious little pupa from the ant community?

"Isn't he with you?" Zoc asked innocently.

"No," Hova replied suspiciously.

"Huh," said Zoc. "Well, that's weird."

"Zoc, what have you done?" Hova asked.

"Me?" he replied. "What did I do?"

"Zoc!" Hova shouted. "Where is he?"

"Gone," Zoc said bluntly.

Hova ran for the door, but Zoc stopped her.

"He led you into a trap, Hova!" Zoc said. "He's blinded you!"

"You're the one who's blinded with hate for humans," Hova said. "I see a young human learning our ways and becoming a part of this colony. I see an *ant*!"

"Impossible!" Zoc scoffed.

"I thought a wizard didn't know such a word," Hova said. She whirled around and stormed out of the chamber. Kreela and Fugax ran to help Hova find Lucas. Even Spindle joined the search.

Zoc's antennae drooped as he realized that he was all alone.

Lucas was also alone as he made his way toward his house. He stopped at a puddle to wash and saw a big black beetle waddling over to him.

"May I?" the beetle asked.

"Help yourself," Lucas said.

"Thanks," the beetle said. "I'm a beetle that loves water, but I'm not a water beetle. Isn't that funny?"

Hilarious, Lucas thought as he continued to wash. Suddenly, he heard a loud *THHHPPP!*

Lucas glanced up. The beetle was gone.

"Oh, well," Lucas said. He leaned over to collect another handful of water and saw two bulgy eyes staring out at him. Before he could run for it, a giant frog leaped out of the water!

"Brraaaaap!" the frog announced, its tongue jutting in and out as fast as lightning. Lucas suddenly knew what had happened to the beetle. And if he didn't escape, the same thing would happen to him!

"Ahhhh!" Lucas screamed, running from the frog. He raced right past Fugax.

"Hey, Lucas!" Fugax called. "I found him!"

At that moment, the frog bounded toward the unaware Fugax.

"Croaker!" Hova shouted.

"This way, Lucas!" Kreela called. She pointed to a giant soda can in the grass.

The ants scurried up the side of the can, but all Lucas could do was hop up and down.

"Concentrate, Lucas!" Hova shouted.

Lucas closed his eyes, gathering his courage and strength. Then he took a deep breath and scurried up the side of the can.

"Come on, Lucas!" Hova cheered. "You can do it!"

Lucas inched his way toward the top. But just as he was nearing it, he began to slip back down.

"Whooaaa!" Lucas cried. He landed with a thump on the ground right in front of the frog!

Lucas stared up at the frog. The frog's tongue whipped out and reeled Lucas in.

"Lucas!" Hova cried.

She turned away, too horrified to look. The big, ugly frog had swallowed her little pupa in a single gulp!

THIRTEEN

After a dark slimy plunge down the frog's gullet, Lucas landed with a splash in its stomach.

"Gross!" Lucas cried.

He was sitting in a pile of muck next to a few of the frog's previous meals.

"We came right down that guy's stomach, didn't we?" the beetle asked.

"Hey, Smiley!" a fly snapped. "You're on my wing!"

"Oh, I am so sorry," the beetle said. "So, what do you guys do?"

"Well, I'm a glowworm. I glow," replied the glowworm sitting next to him.

"That's great!" said the chatty beetle. "Your name and job worked out so perfectly!"

Outside, Zoc suddenly stepped into the path of

the frog and started waving at him, much to the surprise of the other ants.

"What is he doing?" Kreela asked. "Is he crazy?"

"I am delicious," Zoc yelled up to the frog. "Eat me!"

The frog looked down at Zoc and took aim. Zoc closed his eyes and prepared himself for a wild ride as — ZAP — the frog's tongue grabbed him and reeled him in.

"This had better be worth it," Zoc mumbled to himself as he disappeared inside the frog.

The frog's stomach rumbled. Lucas could hear another bug scream as he rode down the frog's throat. His mouth dropped open when he saw that it was Zoc.

"How did you get here?" Lucas asked.

"I sure didn't come through the *rear* entrance," Zoc said.

"Would you quit eating, Fatso?" yelled the grumpy fly. "It's getting cramped down here!"

Just then, Zoc pulled out a brown root and began stirring it in the muck at the bottom of the frog's stomach.

The root began fizzing and foaming. As bubbles popped on the boiling surface, Lucas began to get it. "Hey," he said. "Is that —"

"— an alka root?" Zoc cut in. "So it is."

The fizz filled up the inside of the frog's stomach. Lucas turned to the others and grinned. "Hands in the air!" Lucas shouted.

The frog's eyes bugged out as his throat swelled and he began to shake.

"*BRRRRAAAAAAAAAAAAPPPP!*"

The frog let out a thunderous belch.

The insects shot out of the frog's mouth and through the air. Lucas and Zoc landed side by side in the tall grass.

"Thanks, Zoc," Lucas said. "But why did you do it?"

"An ant will sacrifice himself for his friends," Zoc explained.

"I thought you hated me," Lucas said.

"I didn't do it for you," Zoc said. He glanced back at Hova and smiled. And this time she smiled back!

The ants made their way through the grassy

jungle of the Nickles' yard. They stopped to rest at a giant toadstool. Lucas and Zoc lay stretched out on the top of the toadstool, staring out toward the lights of the city.

"Is this city of yours like a nest?" Zoc asked.

"Kind of," Lucas said.

"Do the humans there work together?" Zoc asked.

"Not everybody," Lucas said. "It's a little more like, you know — every man for himself."

"But that's so primitive," Zoc replied. "How do you get anything done?"

"*Some* people work together," Lucas explained.

"Some?" Zoc asked. "Why not all?"

"I suppose it's because of their differences," Lucas said.

"It is differences that make a colony strong," Zoc said. "Foragers. Scouts. Drones."

Lucas heaved a big sigh. If only that were true on his block!

"My differences just get me beat up," Lucas lamented.

"Like you prefer to beat up ants?" Zoc asked.

Lucas blinked. Zoc's words were a serious reality

check. "I guess I didn't think about what I was doing," he admitted.

"I suppose I, too, can act without thinking. Perhaps in this way we *are* alike." Zoc sighed. "Good night, Lucas."

"Good night, Zoc," Lucas said.

The ants slept peacefully under the stars. But as the sun rose over the toadstool, they were awakened by a loud shout.

"Yai, yai, yai, yai, yai!"

The ants sat up. They saw Fugax, yelling and pointing at the sky.

"I see her!" Fugax exclaimed.

"Who?" Hova asked.

"The Ant Mother!" Fugax said. "She has come!"

Lucas looked up. A giant ant was flying over the grass, just like the painting in the ant cave.

"Wow!" Lucas said. "There really is an Ant Mother!"

But as the ant fluttered closer, Lucas could tell it wasn't a real ant at all. It was a prop on top of the Beals-A-Bug Exterminator van!

"Oh, no!" Lucas murmured.

"Cloud Breather!" Zoc gasped as he saw Stan Beals exit the van.

Lucas's heart sank. He thought he had seen the last of Stan Beals.

"I don't get it!" Lucas cried. "I canceled his contract!"

FOURTEEN

The colony had to be warned.

But when Lucas and his friends reached the ant-hill, the ants were busy celebrating. Word of the Ant Mother had reached the colony before word of the Cloud Breather!

"Praise the Ant Mother," they chanted.

"It's not the Ant Mother!" Zoc shouted. "It is the Cloud Breather!"

"He's come to wipe out the entire colony," Lucas said. "His magic is strong. He's got foggers, sprayers, and zappers!"

"And how do you know of this creature?" the Head of Council asked.

Lucas dropped his head. "Because I brought him here," he said softly.

Silence.

Lucas could see the pained look in Hova's eyes.

"Guards," the Head of Council boomed. "Take this human."

Two soldier ants grabbed Lucas and began dragging him away.

"Let him go!" Hova pleaded.

As Zoc gently pulled Hova back, something caught Lucas's eyes. It was the magic golden elixir in the pouch on Zoc's staff. The one that shrunk him to the size of an ant!

"The potion!" Lucas shouted. "That's it!"

Lucas yelled to Zoc as he was dragged through the crowd. "You shrunk me. You can shrink the Cloud Breather!"

He grabbed a silk squirter from a worker ant. "We can load these things," he said. "And — *POW!* Right in the ear!"

"Perhaps," Zoc said. "But the Cloud Breather towers above us. How do we get close enough?"

Another brainstorm brewed inside Lucas's head. "I've got an idea!" he said.

"Zoc? You would trust this *human*?" the Head of Council asked.

Zoc didn't answer. But Hova smiled and said,

"Sometimes your enemy can become your best friend."

In just minutes, Lucas and Zoc were outside waving frantically in the air.

"Please!" Lucas shouted. "Down here!"

Four wasps dropped from the sky.

"We were just looking for a snack," the wasp leader said with a grin.

Lucas stepped back as he explained the Cloud Breather. "He brings death clouds that will destroy us all — ants *and* wasps," he said. "But we can work together to stop him!"

"Oooh, scary!" the wasp leader joked. "Let's eat!"

The wasps aimed their stingers at Lucas and Zoc.

They were about to strike when an injured wasp crash-landed on the ground. "Sir!" He gasped. "The east nest . . . totally destroyed. We have to get out of here. The cloud is coming!"

Lucas felt the ground rumble. Dozens of insects shot out from the underbrush. A huge cloud billowed behind them!

"Ha, ha, ha!" laughed the voice of Stan Beals.

As hundreds of bugs stampeded, the wasp leader

turned to Lucas. "So, what have you got in mind?" he asked.

Lucas rounded up the troops. Soon an entire wasp fleet stood ready to attack!

"Remember," Lucas called from the back of his wasp. "You get one shot, so don't fire until you see the wax of his ears."

"OK, boys!" the wasp leader called out. "Heat 'em up!"

A dozen wasps beat their wings.

"Hang on!" Lucas shouted. He gripped the wasp's antennae as a blast of wind and leaves whipped around him.

The colony cheered from the top of the anthill.

"That looks like fun!" the beetle said. "Let's help!"

"Why not?" The glowworm sighed. "I only live for two weeks, anyway."

The beetle grabbed the glowworm and the two flew off into the battle.

Back on the ground, Stan sprayed his way toward the anthill. As the wasps buzzed over, he looked up and grinned.

"You want to rumble?" Stan asked. "Come on!"

The ants were good to go.

Kreela and her wasp zoomed toward Stan. She fired her squirter toward his ear but — *ZONK* — headphones deflected it. Then Fugax aimed for Stan's eyes, but a pair of glasses shielded his squirt.

Stan reached out and snatched Fugax's wasp. The wasp tried to sting Stan's hand, but gloves protected him.

"Gee, that hurt!" Stan teased. He flicked his fingers, sending Fugax and the wasps flying across the yard. Then he set his spray can down on the grass.

"He's refilling," Lucas whispered. "Now's our chance."

Zoc zoomed toward Stan. He was about to attack when the exterminator whipped around and blasted him with two cans of bug spray.

"Ahhhh!" Zoc screamed as he crashed behind the bushes.

Lucas boiled with anger as he watched his friend's wasp spiral down toward the ground. He had to do something to exterminate the exterminator!

"Grrr!" Lucas growled as he hovered over Stan. The exterminator swatted the wasp with his cap. Lucas lost his grip on the antennae and tumbled off his wasp, landing on Stan's head.

He was greeted by a blizzard of dandruff and some friendly head lice.

"Hey, nice landing," one louse said. "Uh-oh, he's scratching again."

Lucas zigzagged through a jungle of hair as he dodged Stan's grubby fingernail. He slid down the exterminator's forehead, landing squarely on his greasy nose.

At last, Lucas was in the enemy's face. He stared Stan deep in an eye and shouted at the top of his lungs, "LEAVE MY FRIENDS ALONE!"

FIFTEEN

Stan twitched Lucas off his nose.

"Ahhhhh!" Lucas screamed. The world around him was a dizzying blur as he fell. But just when Lucas thought he was about to hit the ground with a splat, he heard a voice.

"Need a lift?" someone asked.

A wasp swept underneath Lucas, catching him in the nick of time.

Lucas looked back and saw Hova, riding on the wasp. "Thanks!" he said.

Riding the wasp, Lucas and Hova thought they were safe. But then a giant hand brushed behind them.

Lucas and Hova held on tight as the wasp crash-landed and tumbled through the grass. When it came to a stop, Lucas rolled off. But Hova was not as lucky — she was pinned underneath the body of the hulking wasp.

"Hova, are you OK?" Lucas cried.

High above them, Stan blasted his spray can. "Nighty night!" Stan sneered. A massive death cloud rolled across the ground toward Lucas and Hova.

"Get up!" Lucas shouted at the wasp. "We've got to go!"

The cloud was moving in on them. Lucas struggled to roll the wasp off Hova, but it was way too heavy.

"Lucas, go!" Hova said.

In a panic, Lucas darted away from the cloud. But the more he ran, the more he knew what he *really* had to do.

Lucas charged back toward the wasp. He gathered his courage and his strength. Then he slipped under the wasp and lifted him clear off the ground!

"Save yourself!" Hova yelled.

"That's not the way ants are," Lucas replied.

The cloud was gaining on them. Lucas carried the wasp above his head as he and Hova ran toward the safety of a mailbox. Hova scaled the pole. But when she looked down, Lucas was still on the ground.

"Concentrate, Lucas!" Hova called. "Concentrate!"

It was too late. In seconds, the swirling cloud of death engulfed Lucas!

"No!" Hova shouted.

She slumped over the edge of the mailbox. Lucas was her charge. How could she have not protected him? Suddenly, Hova saw someone break through the mist. It was Lucas, climbing the pole with the injured wasp on his back!

"You did it!" Hova cheered.

Two wasps carried away their injured comrade. Zoc flew over on his wasp and they all jumped on.

"I think Lucas just became an ant, Zoc," Hova said with a smile.

But no one smiled when they heard the sound of terrified screams.

"Look!" Lucas pointed to the exterminator stomping toward the anthill. "Stan's headed for the colony!"

"Our weapons are useless." Zoc sighed.

"We just need a clear shot," Lucas said. He looked around and noticed a wasp's stinger. "Hey, wait. A *shot*!"

The ants put Lucas's new plan into action.

"I've never attacked anyone before," the beetle said. "Isn't that funny?"

"A riot." The glowworm sighed.

The glowworm and the beetle flew toward Stan. As they got closer, they saw a round hole in his pant leg.

"Here's a way in," the beetle said.

The insects zipped through the hole and up the pant leg. They came to a stop when they reached the meaty part of Stan's thigh.

"Perfect!" the beetle said. He opened his maw and took a big bite out of the exterminator's leg.

"Owwww!" Stan screamed.

Lucas smiled as Stan doubled over in pain. "Now, let's give this human a good-bye kiss," Lucas said.

Their wasp shot forward, his stinger covered with the golden elixir. Zoc, Hova, and Lucas held tight as the pointy stinger rammed right into Stan's butt!

"Yeeeeeooooowwwwww!" Stan screamed.

Ants cheered. The lower part of Stan's body began shrinking to half its size.

Finally, it was payback time. Swarms of wasps and insects chased Stan as he ran for a tricycle.

"You haven't seen the last of me," Stan shouted as he pedaled away. "I'll be baaaaaaaaack!"

"Praise the Mother!" Lucas cheered.

"For a human, you make a pretty good ant," Zoc told Lucas.

The Ant Council thought so, too.

"I no longer see a human among ants, but a single colony," the Queen said as everyone gathered to honor Lucas. "No more Lucas the Destroyer. Now, you are Rokai the Ant!"

"It's an ant name," Hova said proudly.

"A wizard name," Zoc added.

Lucas smiled. He was an ant at last!

He was Rokai!

"Rokai has earned his freedom," the Queen said. "And we have earned a friend."

Lucas heard a voice inside his head. It was Zoc sending him a telepathic message!

"I thought it was impossible to call a human 'friend,'" Zoc transmitted.

"A wizard knows no such word," Lucas sent back. Then he walked over to Hova and gave her a big hug.

"I'm going to miss you, Hova," Lucas said.

"I'll miss you, too, Lucas," Hova said. "Cross my heart."

Lucas laughed as the whole colony crossed their bulbous butts. The good-natured ants had become almost like a family to him. But now it was time to return to his real family.

It was time to go home.

SIXTEEN

"He's back! He's back!" Mommo cried. She peered through her binoculars as Lucas grew larger and larger in the front yard.

Lucas was happy to be home. He was even happier when his parents' car pulled into the driveway.

"Hey, Mom!" Lucas shouted as he ran outside. He hugged his mom tight and didn't let go.

"Lucas?" Doreen asked. "What is it?"

"I forgot to tell you good-bye," Lucas said. "Good-bye."

Doreen hugged him back, noticing the change in her son. "Good-bye to you, too."

Fred Nickle hauled a huge suitcase into the house. "Casa, sweet casa!" he declared.

Lucas was about to follow his mom and dad inside when he heard a familiar voice.

"Hey, Pukas!" Steve called. "Where've you been, buddy? We've been looking for you."

Lucas groaned as he turned around. He had almost forgotten about Steve and his pathetic gang of goons.

The kids advanced on Lucas. Then suddenly, Nicky noticed Lucas's Frog Flyer T-shirt.

"Oh, cool," Nicky babbled. "Frog Flyers! You play?"

Steve punched Nicky, but he and the other kids didn't seem to notice.

"Yeah, I play," Lucas replied.

"Do you play the online version?" one of the kids asked.

"You mean CyberFrog Seven?" Lucas asked.

Steve glared angrily at his crew.

"Do *all* you idiots want to be dog-piled?" he asked menacingly. "Huh?"

"Hey!" Lucas interjected. "Leave them alone. What the craznox is wrong with you?"

"Oh, look!" Steve mocked. "Pukas is a big man. Ya know, if I were you, I'd be worrying about myself."

Lucas stepped in front of the other kids, facing Steve.

"That's not the way friends are," Lucas said bravely.

"Dog pile!" Steve commanded as he lunged toward Lucas. But there was no response from the other kids.

"I said, *DOG PILE*!" Steve yelled again.

The other kids looked at Lucas and smiled as if they were all in on the same joke. Then they all turned to Steve.

"Dog pile!" they shouted.

"Ahhhh!" Steve screamed. For the first time in his bully career, he was not the bully.

The kids raced toward Steve, chasing him down the street.

Meanwhile, back in the anthill, Hova and Zoc were reminiscing about Rokai.

"They sure grow up fast," Hova said with a sigh.

"Heh, heh, heh," Zoc said with a sneaky laugh.

"What?" Hova asked suspiciously.

"Look what I've got," Zoc said, playfully waving a dandelion thistle in front of Hova.

"Oh, no!" Hova cried. "Zoc, wait! I'm serious. Ha, ha, ha, ha!"

Zoc tickled Hova with the dandelion as Spindle danced happily around them.

Suddenly, up above them, a huge shadow covered the sun.

The ants looked up to see a giant Lucas, pouring dozens of jelly beans onto the ground.

Fugax and Kreela raced toward the pile.

"Yai, yai, yai, yai, yai!" they cried. "Thanks, Lucas!"

"Anytime," Lucas replied. "That's just the way friends are."